High Time in New York

Penn Mullin

High Noon Books
Novato, California

Cover Design and Interior Illustrations: Damon Rarey

International Standard Book Number: 0-87879-960-5

10 09 08 07 06 05 04 03
5 4 3 2 1 0 9 8 7

You'll enjoy all the High Noon Books. Write for
a free full list of titles.

Contents

All aboard! Juan; Mike, their van driver; Justin; Miss Lake, their teacher; Amy; and Lisa smile for the camera before taking off on their trip.

When Miss Lake's seventh grade class entered the President's *See America the Beautiful* contest, they didn't think they had a chance to win. It was fun thinking they might, so everyone wrote and sent in a short essay on "What Do You Like Best About Being an American?"

They could hardly believe it when the letter came. It said: "The essays sent in by four members of your class were outstanding. These students have won a three-week trip across the United States with their teacher. All expenses will be paid."

The class clapped when Miss Lake finished reading the letter and Lisa, Amy, Justin, and Juan went home to pack their bags.

CHAPTER 1

Welcome to Manhattan

"We're not moving! We're stuck! Look at all those cars around us," Juan said.

"New York City has seven million people," Miss Lake said.

"And they're all outside our van!" Lisa said.

"We're very near the Empire State Building," said their teacher, Miss Lake. "Look out the windows. The Empire State Building is quite a sight."

"Wow! How high is it?" Amy asked.

"One hundred and two stories, or one thousand two hundred twenty four feet," Miss Lake said. "One thousand four hundred fifty-four feet if you count the lightning rod!"

"There must be four thousand windows," Lisa guessed.

"Six thousand five hundred," Miss Lake said. "How would you like to wash those?"

"The van is moving!" Justin said. "At last!"

"I see our stop just ahead." Miss Lake pointed out the window.

"Are we going to the top of the Empire State Building?" Lisa asked.

"The deck on the 102nd floor has been

2

closed for some time. But there is another deck on the 86th floor, over 1,000 feet above the city" Miss Lake said.

The van stopped. Everybody was glad to get out. They had been sitting a long time.

"Thanks, Mike. We'll meet you here at five," Miss Lake told the van driver.

"Have fun! Don't get dizzy up there," Mike said,

"I'm feeling dizzy already," Lisa said. "And I'm not even on the elevator yet!"

"Follow me," Miss Lake said. She led the kids off the van. They followed the crowds of people. Everyone was going to the Empire State Building.

There were lots of shops, banks, and restaurants, and even a post office, inside the Empire State Building.

"This is like a mini-city in here," Amy said. "Look at all these neat stores!"

"I'm saving my money. Let's head to the top," said Justin.

"There are the elevators," Lisa said.

Everybody bought a ticket, and then got into an elevator.

"Hold on! We're going to the 80th floor in just 45 seconds!"

"I think I just left my stomach on the ground," Justin said.

"We're here!" said Juan. "That was fast."

Everyone walked outside. They were in a glassed-in room.

"Look at the view!" Miss Lake said. "You can see New York and four other states from here."

"What is that big building to the East?" Amy asked. "The one by the river."

"That's the United Nations," Miss Lake said. "The world's meeting house. People from many countries go there. They work to make peace and get help with problems. We'll visit it tomorrow. We can even watch some meetings."

"Is that where they have the magic earphones?" Lisa asked.

"Yes, We can listen to people talk in

different languages. The earphones change these languages into English," said Miss Lake.

"Look, the Statue of Liberty!" Justin cried. "Hey Lisa, you've got to come see it."

Lisa was standing back away from the side. She started slowly towards the other kids.

"You know I can't look down," she said.

"Just look to the South," said Juan.

"How are you doing, Lisa?" Miss Lake asked.

"So far, so good." Lisa smiled. "I'm just looking to the South."

"How would you like to stay here overnight?" Miss Lake said.

"Can we?" Justin asked.

The Most Famous Skyline in the World.

Well, first you have to join the Boy Scouts, or the Girl Scouts," Miss Lake said as she looked at Lisa. "They let Scout troops camp here a few times a year."

"No thanks," said Lisa.

"I heard that there are lights on the outside of the building that they turn on at night," Justin said.

"That's right," said Miss Lake. "The first light was turned on in 1932, one year after the Empire State Building was built. They say that the light could be seen for 50 miles."

"Wow!" said Juan. I didn't think the Empire State Building was that old."

"Now they use several hundred lights, with

different colors." Miss Lake continued.

"Do they turn them all on at the same time?" Amy asked.

"They use certain colors for special days. For example, they turn on the red, white, and blue lights for the fourth of July," Miss Lake said.

"I bet even the birds like looking at the Empire State Building with the lights on," Amy said.

"Yes, and no," Miss Lake said. The birds like flying toward the lights, but sometimes they hit the Empire State Building."

"The poor birds!" Amy said.

"Don't worry, Amy," Miss Lake said. "They

9

turn off the lights on cloudy or foggy nights when the building is hard to see."

"Let's walk around up here. I want to see more of the city," Juan said.

"I see Central Park," Lisa said. "It is totally huge!"

"We'll go there later. It has a zoo, a lake, stables, even a castle!" said Miss Lake.

"We need a whole week in New York City," Justin said. "When we won this trip, I never dreamed we would see so many new things. We are all lucky."

"You're right. There's so much to see. But you can come back. You can spend more time on things you like," Miss Lake said.

"Juan's starting to look dizzy. Remember, he and Lisa get that way in high places," Justin said.

"Time to start down," said Miss Lake. "Line up for the elevator! We have a ferry to catch for the Statue of Liberty!"

CHAPTER 2

Liberty Island

"We made it! The ferry leaves from right over there," Miss Lake told the kids. "Lisa and Juan, are you feeling better now?"

"Much better on the ground," Lisa said.

"Are you ready to get on a boat?" Justin laughed.

"It's not a long way," Miss Lake said. "But it looks stormy. I hope the ride won't be choppy."

"We'll be OK, don't worry," said Juan.

"Here comes the ferry now," said Miss Lake. "Let's walk down to the dock."

"I can't believe it! That's the Statue of Liberty out there!" Amy said. She looked out over the water.

"Come on, Amy. You'll miss the boat," Juan yelled. Lots of people were crowding aboard.

"I'm coming," Amy called out. She followed the other kids onto the boat.

"Wow, it sure is rough!" Justin said. "Look at those waves." Water was splashing up onto the dock. The wind was blowing hard.

Miss Lake and the kids stood out on the deck. The boat pulled away from the dock.

"You'll get a great view of Manhattan now," Miss Lake said. "You can see all the skyscrapers."

"Where did the word Manhattan come from?" Juan asked her.

"It came from the Algonquins. They were the Native Americans who first lived here," said Miss Lake. "They called this place Manhatoor, Island of the Hills."

"It's hard to believe it's an island," said Justin. "It's so big."

"The guidebook says Manhattan is 13½ miles long," Miss Lake said. "But it is only about 2½ miles wide!"

"Hey! Who's rocking the boat?" Amy

asked. She held tightly to the railing.

"This is getting rough!" Juan said.

"Has one of these boats ever sunk?" Lisa asked.

"Look, isn't that beautiful?" Miss Lake pointed back to the skyline of the city.

"It looks peaceful from here," Juan said. "But then you get in the middle of it—and wow! Millions of people and cars."

"Welcome to Liberty Island," a voice over the loudspeaker said. "Go straight ahead to the Statue of Liberty. Please be careful as you leave the ferry. The water is very rough today."

Miss Lake and the kids lined up to get off.

"That was a quick trip," said Amy.

"Hey—check out the Statue of Liberty!" Juan opened his guidebook. "One hundred and fifty-two feet high! And she's on a base that's just about as high!"

"Are we taking the elevator? Or are we walking all the way up?" asked Miss Lake.

"Walking!" everybody shouted.

"I heard you can feel the statue sway in the wind," Justin said.

"That's a scary thought today." Miss Lake looked up at the sky. It was full of dark clouds. "I'm worried about a storm."

"I lift my lamp—beside the golden door."

CHAPTER 3

Up to the Crown

The wind roared. Miss Lake and the kids lined up at the Statue of Liberty.

"We'll be inside in a minute," Juan said.

"Are you sure you want to walk up?" Miss Lake asked.

"Yes," the kids all said together.

"It's only 344 steps up to her crown." Justin was looking in Juan's guidebook.

"Only!" laughed Miss Lake. "And with that wind roaring all around us!"

"Can you believe this? Liberty's fingernails are each a foot across!" Justin read aloud.

"And her mouth is 3 feet wide!" Juan said.

The line moved ahead. Miss Lake and the kids got inside the doorway.

"We take the elevator to the top of the base," Lisa said. "Then we walk."

"First let's talk about Liberty. Who knows where she came from?" asked Miss Lake.

"France?" Amy asked.

"Right. She was a gift from France in 1876. Her sculptor was Frederic A. Bartholdi. He molded Liberty's face after his mother's. Does anybody know what Liberty is made of?" asked Miss Lake.

"Stone?" Juan asked.

"No, copper. That's why she has that bluish-green color. Copper is lighter than stone but still strong," Miss Lake told them. "Remember, Liberty had to come to this country by boat!"

"How did they do that?" Lisa asked. "She's so huge!"

"They took the statue apart in France. They put each piece of her body into a box," said Miss Lake. "An ear and a curl in one box. Her mouth and eyes in another. Then the boxes were put on a boat in France."

"So they put Liberty back together over here?" Lisa asked.

"Like one totally giant puzzle," Justin said

20

with a laugh.

"Yes. Think of all the pieces for her robe!" Miss Lake said.

"It's our turn to go up now," Juan said. "Here's the elevator."

"Lead on," Miss Lake said. "I'm glad we get to ride a little," she laughed.

They all rode the elevator to the top of the base. Then they started up the stairs. The steps were steep. They kept going around and around.

"Don't get dizzy, Lisa!" Justin yelled.

"No problem. There's no way I can look down," Lisa said.

"Listen to that wind," Amy said. "Really sounds spooky."

"Wait till we get up to the crown," Justin said. "This is nothing."

"How are you doing, Miss Lake?" Amy called out.

"I'm coming. This is my workout for the week!" their teacher said.

"Ooooh! Can you feel this thing sway?" Amy held on tight to the railing.

"Do they ever close the statue in high winds?" Lisa asked.

"Maybe we should go back down." Amy's voice was shaky.

The wind howled around the statue. The kids climbed higher.

CHAPTER 4

A Warning

"I think we're getting close," Juan called out.

"I've been counting. We're at 300 steps!" Lisa said.

"We must be in her neck now. These stairs are getting smaller. This isn't made for linebackers," Justin laughed.

"Miss Lake, still coming?" Amy called down the stairs.

"I'm here!" Her voice sounded far away.

The wind was louder than ever.

"Feel this thing move!" Juan shouted.

"I think I want to go down," Amy said.

"We're almost there. Just a few more steps," Justin told her.

"Hang in there," Lisa said. "If I can do it, you can."

Suddenly they heard a shout. "Here's the top! We're at the crown!" It was Juan.

"Just wait till he looks down," Justin laughed.

The last few stairs were a tight squeeze. Then they were up in the crown. There were windows all around it. Only two other people were there. They were an older man and woman. They smiled at the kids.

"Wow, check out that view!" Juan said.

"Hey, here comes Miss Lake," Justin called out.

"You did great!" Juan told her.

"I'm here! That's what counts," Miss Lake laughed. "And we haven't blown away yet."

Just then a blast of wind hit the crown.

"I think I spoke too soon," Miss Lake said.

The crown shook. Another blast of wind hit it hard. The woman screamed.

"It's OK, Ruth. Don't worry," said the man with her.

"This statue is used to strong winds," Juan said. "That's what my guidebook says."

"She's even been in hurricanes," said Justin.

"That's right. She has stood here a long time," Miss Lake said. "She had her hundredth birthday in 1986. What a party that was! There were super fireworks. Boats had a big parade all around her."

The wind roared outside the crown.

Suddenly a loudspeaker came on.

"Ladies and gentlemen, please listen carefully. We are having very high winds. Do not start down the stairs. Wait until we say it is safe. Stay in the crown. Don't worry. The statue is very strong. I repeat: Do not start down the stairs."

CHAPTER 5

High Winds

The loudspeaker clicked off. There was silence. Then the wind began to howl. The crown shook. The man and woman held on to each other tightly.

"I'm really scared," said Amy.

"Think if we were up in the torch," Justin said. "Boy, I bet it's shaking up there!"

Another blast of wind shook the crown.

"Remember all the steel inside this statue," Miss Lake said. "She is strong."

The man and woman were talking softly.

"We shouldn't have come up here, Paul," the woman said.

"But we wanted to, remember? Because of Mother and Dad," Paul said.

"You're right, but I'm scared," Ruth told her brother.

"I'm sure we'll get to go down soon." Miss Lake smiled at Ruth and Paul.

"I hope you're right," Paul said. "We climbed up here for a special reason. Our parents came to America from Poland in 1915. They first saw this statue from the deck of a ship."

"They always talked about that day,"

Mary said. "They had waited so long to get to America. They had saved up all their money to come."

"They had no freedom in Poland. But here they could start their own store. They had a clothing store in New York for fifty years," Paul said.

"I can understand why this is a special place for you to visit," Miss Lake said. "When your parents got off the ship, did they have to go to Ellis Island?"

"Yes. They had to stay there for two weeks," Ruth said.

"My mother was so sick. So they made her wait. You couldn't come into America until you were well," Paul said.

"I bet that was hard," Lisa said. "After all that time on the ship."

"It was. Mother told us a lot about Ellis Island. It was not a happy time for her," Paul said.

"We want to go see the museum there," Ruth said. "If we ever get down from here!"

The wind slammed hard against the crown. The walls shook.

"I'm ready for this to stop. Right now," said Amy.

"Hey, maybe it isn't all bad. We might be on the news tonight! Stuck on top of the Statue of Liberty," Justin laughed.

"You would laugh about anything," said Lisa.

"Hey, I've got some trivia questions for you all. I bet you can't guess the answers to these!" Miss Lake said.

"Try us," Juan said.

"OK. Here's the first one. How long is Liberty's nose?" Miss Lake asked.

"Six feet," Justin said.

"Three," said Paul.

"Any more guesses?" asked Miss Lake.

"No? OK, it's 4½ feet long," Miss Lake said. "Here's another one. Liberty carries stone tablets in her hand. What is written on them?"

"Some numbers?" asked Juan.

"Yes. Do you know which ones?" Miss Lake asked him.

Juan looked out the window. He tried to read the numbers on the tablets.

"I think it's a date," he said. "But the numbers look funny. Sort of like a different language."

"You are right. It *is* a date. It is written in Roman numerals: July IV, MDCCLXXVI, or 1776. Who knows what happened on that date?" Miss Lake asked.

"The Declaration of Independence," Amy said. "It was signed then. America said it was not part of England anymore."

"Right, Amy. So Liberty is telling people

that there is freedom in America."

Suddenly they felt the statue sway.

"Ooooh! I hate that," Amy cried. "When is this going to end?"

"Look at the waves out there!" Justin looked down at the water.

"I wonder if the ferries have stopped running," Lisa said.

"More trivia questions please," Ruth asked Miss Lake. "It helps us not to think about the storm."

"OK. Here we go." Miss Lake opened her guidebook. "How long is Liberty's arm?"

"Fifty feet," guessed Ruth.

"Forty," said Justin.

"Longer than you think. It's 46 feet," Miss Lake told them.

"We were close," Ruth laughed.

"How many spikes in Liberty's crown?" Miss Lake asked.

"Four," Paul guessed.

"Eight," said Lisa.

"There are seven," Miss Lake told them. "Liberty's light shines on seven seas and seven continents."

The wind roared around the statue.

Then suddenly everything was quiet again. No one spoke.

Finally Juan said, "I think the wind has stopped."

"But it will start up again. I know it will," said Amy.

Everybody stayed quiet. Everybody just listened for the wind.

Suddenly the loudspeaker came on.

"It is safe to start down now. Please come down right away. The wind may start again. We want to get you down fast. Please be careful on the stairs."

"We're coming!" Juan shouted. "Right away!"

"Not Amy. She wants to stay a little longer," Justin laughed.

Amy chased Justin over to the stairs.

On the way to Ellis Island

CHAPTER 6

The Door to America

"It feels good to be down!" Amy said. She looked up at Liberty's crown.

"I'm still swaying," Lisa said.

Ruth and Paul came up to the group.

"We're glad you were with us up there. You helped the time pass faster. And we sure learned a lot, Miss Lake!" Paul said.

"Call me Carol. We're glad you were with us, too. Are you going to Ellis Island now?" Miss Lake asked.

"We'll take the next ferry," Ruth said.

"So will we. But we'll look at this poem first," Miss Lake said. She called the kids.

"I want to show you a special poem," she told them. "It was written in the 1880's." The poem was on the base of the statue.

"Who wrote it?" Juan asked.

"Emma Lazarus, a New York poet," Miss Lake said. "Listen:

Give me your tired, your poor,

Your huddled masses

yearning to breathe free,

..........I lift my lamp

beside the golden door!

"What great words! Liberty is welcoming

people to America," Miss Lake said. "Think how happy the immigrants were to see her. Remember Ruth and Paul's parents. They had spent a long time on a ship."

"What other countries did people come from?" Justin asked.

"All over. France, Germany, Russia, Mexico, many Asian countries. Most came for freedom and a better life," Miss Lake said. "We'll learn more about them at Ellis Island. Let's head for the ferry."

Everybody started over to the dock. Then they got on the ferry. Ruth and Paul stood on the deck with the group. They all looked back at the Statue of Liberty.

"Tonight we will see her torch lighted," Paul said. "The lights are 2,500 times brighter than full moonlight. They can be seen far out to sea."

"Her torch is painted gold. The lights shine up at it," Ruth told them.

"Liberty really is beautiful," Amy said. "I'll never forget today."

"We have to check the news tonight. We might be on it," Justin said.

"Still hoping, aren't you?" laughed Lisa.

"Look over at New York," Miss Lake said. "What a splendid city!"

"Where does the name New York come from? You already told us about Manhattan,"

Justin said.

"The Dutch explorer Henry Hudson called it New Amsterdam. That was in 1625. Later, English settlers named it New York. They wanted to honor the Duke of York," Miss Lake said.

"Look, we're going to dock," Amy said. "Quick trip!"

"Welcome to Ellis Island," the loudspeaker said. "Follow the signs to the Great Hall. The next ferry leaves at four."

"Pretend you are an immigrant," Miss Lake told the kids. "You just got off the boat from Italy. You are tired, dirty, hungry. Now you must wait in long lines. You must be checked. If you are sick, you have to stay here."

They all got off the ferry. Then they walked into a huge building.

"This was the Great Hall," Paul told them. "Here you waited in long lines."

"Our mother told us the noise was awful," Ruth said. "So many languages. And so many questions. Questions like what is your age? What work can you do? How much money do you have?"

"Sometimes people's names got changed here," Paul said. "An immigrant said his name was Hoffmanstall. It got written down as Hoffman. Then that was the man's new name in America."

"Pretty scary," said Justin.

"I bet some of you have family from other countries," Miss Lake said. "Maybe they came through Ellis Island. Maybe it was a great-grandmother. Or a great-uncle."

"I do! My great-grandfather came from Italy. He must have been here," Lisa said.

"My grandparents came from China," said Amy. "Their boat went to San Francisco."

"When you get home, try to find out what country your family came from," Miss Lake said. "You can learn a lot from older people in your family."

"I've got an idea," Ruth said. "Tonight our

New York family is giving a party. There will be Polish dances, Polish food. We want all of you to come. How about it?"

"It sounds great!" Miss Lake said.

"Thank you!" all the kids said at once.

"We'll make everybody guess how we met you," Paul laughed. "They'll never believe it!"

"Come on! The Great Hall tour is starting," Ruth said.

Miss Lake turned to Lisa.

"Lisa it's your turn to write a postcard to send to our school. You are going to have so much to write about."

"I know," Lisa laughed. "I may need two postcards!"